DOZENS OF ZOMBIES WERE MARCHING ALONG THE DOCKS.

They came from alleyways and houses. Some even came off ships. All were following the sound of the Cobweb Queen's flute.

Horrified, Otto, Uncle Tooth, and Olivia made their way past the zombies to the jail. The bars on Doodle's cell had been bent back. Doodle and Auntie Hick were gone!

They ran outside. By now, the line of zombies had reached the edge of town. It was disappearing into Mookey Swamp. One especially large zombie was carrying Auntie Hick.

"We've got to stop them!" screamed Otto.

STEP INTO READING BOOKS™
BY GEOFFREY HAYES:

The Curse of the Cobweb Queen
The Mystery of the Pirate Ghost
The Secret of Foghorn Island
The Treasure of the Lost Lagoon

SWAMP
OF THE
HIDEOUS
ZOMBIES

BY GEOFFREY HAYES

A FIRST STEPPING STONE BOOK

Random House 🏠 New York

Library of Congress Cataloging-in-Publication Data
Hayes, Geoffrey.
Swamp of the Hideous Zombies / by Geoffrey Hayes.
p. cm. "A First Stepping Stone book."
SUMMARY: When a creepy fortune-teller moves into Boogle Bay and one by one
people begin to disappear, Otto feels sure zombie monsters are at work.
ISBN 0-679-87696-0 (trade) — 0-679-97696-5 (lib. bdg.)
[1. Monsters—Fiction.   2. Horror stories.]   I. Title.
PZ7.H31455Sw   1996   [E]—dc20   96-883

Printed in the United States of America   10 9 8 7 6 5 4 3 2 1

Random House, Inc.   New York, Toronto, London, Sydney, Auckland

http://www.randomhouse.com/

CONTENTS

THE GRAVEYARD CREEPER

Did I scare you? Folks around here know me as the "Graveyard Creeper." I'm always creeping around, digging up gory little epics. Like this one, which I call *Swamp of the Hideous Zombies.*

Zombies aren't really so bad. My brother was a zombie—at least during school hours. He got straight "C's" on his report card. "C" for "corpse," that is. Heh, heh!

But these zombies are clearly up to no good. They give our heroes, Otto and Olivia, quite a few scares. In fact, this story is so scary, it would give a ghost goose bumps! So you'd better keep your eyes open, look over your shoulder every so often, and remember...it's only a story.

Or is it?

1
ZOMBIES IN BOOGLE BAY

Otto raced inside the general store, slammed the door, and pulled the shade down.

He didn't stop to say hello to Uncle Tooth or to his cousin, Olivia, who were standing at the counter. He went right to the magazine rack and grabbed the latest copy of *Monsters and Ghouls*.

Quickly, Otto looked through the pages.

"What's *his* problem?" Olivia asked Uncle Tooth.

"Here it is! I knew it!" cried Otto.

He pointed to a drawing of a huge, bug-eyed figure with matted hair. At the bottom, in bold type, was the word ZOMBIE.

"I just saw one of these by the movie theater."

"You saw a zombie?" Uncle Tooth cried.

"Are you sure it wasn't just your reflection in a window?" said Olivia.

"Be serious!" said Otto. "I was looking at the poster for *Invasion of the Crawlee Things*. Then this huge, bug-eyed creep came marching along."

"It was probably late for the movie," said Olivia.

Otto closed the magazine. "If you don't want to hear my story...fine! But you'll be sorry."

"I want to hear it," said Uncle Tooth.

Otto continued. "I saw the monster head

down an alley and stop in front of an old lady. I thought it was going to eat her! Then I saw she was *talking* to it. She pointed toward the beach. The monster nodded and marched off."

"Well, I'm terrified!" Olivia said.

Uncle Tooth handed Olivia a roll of film. "I can help you load your camera, if you like."

"Thanks, but I know how to do it," she said.

"That's okay! Just ignore me!" cried Otto.

Uncle Tooth lit his pipe. "What made you think it was a monster?" he asked.

"It looked like one," said Otto.

"Then why wasn't the old lady afraid?"

"I don't know. Maybe she's controlling it."

"Maybe your imagination is running away with you," said Uncle Tooth. He opened the door. "You were probably spooked by the movie poster and thought you saw—"

"No! It *was* a zombie!" cried Otto. He quickly replaced the magazine and followed Uncle Tooth and Olivia out of the store.

Outside, they saw Auntie Hick coming toward them, looking worried.

"Have any of you seen Ducky Doodle?" she asked.

"I saw him about twenty minutes ago. He was digging on the beach," said Uncle Tooth.

"Well, he's not there now," Auntie Hick went on. "I found his pail and shovel...but no Doodle! I wouldn't let him go treasure hunting until he cleaned up his room. He was angry and stomped around. Then he got awfully quiet. When I went to check on him, the window was open and Doodle was gone."

"Maybe the zombie got him!" said Otto.

"Zombie?" cried Auntie Hick.

"Pay no attention, Auntie Hick," said Olivia. "Otto's trying to annoy me because I wouldn't be in his stupid Monster Club."

"Excuse me?" said Otto. "I wouldn't *let* you join....Remember?"

Otto had come up with the idea of a club for studying and learning about monsters. He had decided he wouldn't allow any girls to join. But he was miffed when Olivia wasn't at all interested.

Uncle Tooth told Otto and Olivia to stop bickering. Then he promised Auntie Hick that if he found Ducky Doodle, he'd be sure to send him home. She hurried off.

"I'll bet the old lady and the zombie have something to do with this," said Otto.

"It's not the first time Doodle has disappeared," said Uncle Tooth. "He'll turn up."

"Well, I have more important things to do than to chase dumb monsters," Olivia told them.

"Like what?" Otto said.

"My dad sent me this camera with a built-in flash. I'm going to take some really good photos and sell them to the *Boogle Bay Bugle.*"

"Now, *that's* dumb! Who'd pay money for your old pictures?" Otto laughed. "What are you going to photograph…little kitties?"

"I'm not talking to you anymore," said Olivia. She walked away.

Otto scowled at her. "I can't wait until she leaves Boogle Bay!" he muttered.

2
THE SECRET OF 1313

Olivia was spoiling Otto's summer!

She had arrived right after school ended and wouldn't be going home until the end of August. She was staying with Ducky Doodle and Auntie Hick.

Otto didn't mind Olivia in small doses, but she was too pushy.

When he found an old boat on the beach, Olivia insisted on helping repair it.

When he built a fort under the pier, Olivia had to build one, too.

She even got Uncle Tooth to help, so her

fort would be fancier than Otto's.

"I thought you liked your cousin," said Uncle Tooth. He and Otto were on their way home to Lone Point.

"She's okay," said Otto. "The trouble is, she's always butting into things. But when *she* wants to do something, does she invite me? No!"

Uncle Tooth frowned. "Maybe she's waiting for you to invite her first."

Otto made a face. "Then I'd *never* get rid of her! You believe me about the zombie, don't you, Uncle Tooth?"

"I believe in zombies," Uncle Tooth said. "I had dealings with them years ago. Nasty things, zombies! But just because the person you saw *looked* like a zombie, it doesn't mean that it *was* a zombie. You need more evidence."

"I'll get some," said Otto. "This can be the

first case for my Monster Club!"

As soon as he got home, Otto ran to his room and got his telescope. That was for spying on the zombie.

He found a pad and pencil. They were for writing down important information.

Finally, he reached under his pillow, grabbed his Good-Luck Pebble, and stuffed it in his pocket. That was for protection.

Otto wished he had Olivia's camera, but there was no point in asking to use it. She'd only say no.

"Wait until I prove my zombie theory," thought Otto. "That'll show her!"

The day was turning overcast, with an eerie light in the sky. Otto went to the end of the boardwalk, where Ducky Doodle liked to hang out. He searched in the sand for clues, but couldn't find anything.

He noticed Mr. Sedley Mether sitting on a high rock. Sedley had a sketchbook propped in his lap. He kept glancing across the bay, then bending his head to draw.

"I'll ask Sedley if he's seen anything fishy," thought Otto.

As he neared the high rock, Otto saw a tall, thin figure come up behind Sedley.

It was the old lady he had seen with the zombie!

Quickly, Otto hid in some tall grass. He peered through his telescope. The old lady was talking to Sedley. Then she handed him something and moved away.

The old lady passed Otto as she headed back toward the boardwalk. Otto was eager to follow her. But he was just as eager to know what she had said to Sedley Mether.

The instant she was out of sight, Otto

climbed the path up to the big rock.

"Hello, Sedley," he called.

"Hello, Otto. Want to see my sketch?"

"Very nice...say, Sedley, what did that old lady want?"

"She said I was an excellent artist," said Sedley Mether. "She wanted me to paint her portrait. I told her I'm much better at flowers. But she offered me a lot of money. So I'm thinking about it."

"What did she give you?"

Sedley reached in his pocket and handed Otto a business card.

Otto read the card.

"MADAME WEBSTER, FORTUNE-TELLER. FREE READING— ONE DAY ONLY! 1313 TRIANGULAR SQUARE, BOOGLE BAY"

"It really says 'Free Reading'?" asked Sedley.

"Yes," said Otto. "But I don't trust that old lady. I'd stay away from her, if I were you."

He wrote the address in his notepad before returning the card to Sedley. This was his first clue! Otto scrambled down the rock, full of excitement.

Otto just knew that 1313 Triangular Square was linked to the zombie, and that the zombie was linked to Ducky Doodle. But he wasn't sure how. He was going to check out the address and get some evidence.

Triangular Square was in the bad section of town. Otto didn't come here very often. The buildings were old. Some were even deserted, with broken windows and boarded-up doors. Otto clutched his Good-Luck Pebble.

Suddenly, he heard a CLICK!

A familiar voice said, "Hey, you bozo,

you ruined my picture!"

"Olivia! What are you doing here?" gasped Otto.

"I thought if the newspaper published photos of these old buildings, people might want to fix them up."

"But what are you doing *here?*" Otto insisted.

"Oh. After I left you, I met an old lady who gave me this card. It says she's telling fortunes free," said Olivia.

"Are you crazy?" Otto cried. "That's the old lady with the zombie! She's probably handing those out to everybody."

"So? What's the big—?"

Otto shushed her. The door of 1313 was opening!

Otto and Olivia ducked behind a garbage can.

Ducky Doodle walked out. There was a blank look in his eyes. The old lady followed. She was saying something to him.

Doodle nodded, then walked stiffly down the street. The old lady glanced around before going back inside.

"I knew it!" whispered Otto. "She's turned him into a zombie!"

"I don't know," Olivia whispered back. "Doodle always looks blank."

"We've got to follow him," said Otto.

"*You* follow him," Olivia said. "I want to get pictures of that shop. I can see the headlines now: FAKE FORTUNE-TELLER EXPOSED!"

"We don't know she's a fake. She could be hypnotizing people," said Otto. "Anyway, this is *my* investigation."

"Oh, do you *own* it? Look! Ducky Doodle's getting away!"

Otto sighed. There was Olivia, trying to run things again. But he was curious about Doodle. So he just said, "Be careful," and ran off.

Otto was afraid he'd lost Doodle. Then he saw him crossing the old trolley line. "Doodle," he said. "Are you all right?"

Ducky Doodle did not look at Otto. He kept marching along, staring straight ahead. "Must find treasure," he said.

"What treasure?" asked Otto.

"Must find treasure."

"Did that old lady put you up to this?"

"Must find treasure."

Otto knew he wasn't going to get any clear answers from Doodle. He would just have to follow him closely and see where he ended up.

3
MADAME WEBSTER

Meanwhile, Olivia was sneaking up on 1313 Triangular Square. The window shade was drawn. But she found a little space at the bottom to peek through.

It was dark inside. Where had the old lady gone?

Suddenly, a voice behind her said, "And just what do you think you're doing?"

Olivia spun around and came face to face with Madame Webster!

"Y-you gave me this card," she said. She held it up.

Madame Webster's sour look changed to a sly smile.

"So I did. Is that a camera around your neck?" she asked, drawing closer. "I don't like cameras. They make nosy people even nosier. You aren't planning on taking any pictures around here, arc you?"

Madame Webster pressed Olivia against the door of the shop.

"Just one!" cried Olivia. She flashed her camera in Madame Webster's face.

Madame Webster blinked her eyes and screamed: "Clegg! Clegg! Come here! I need you!"

The shop door opened. Standing there was a large, hulking figure with wild, matted hair. Clegg was a zombie, too!

"Get the brat's camera!" ordered Madame Webster.

Clegg lunged for Olivia, but she squirmed out of the way. She gave Clegg a swift kick on the shins before tearing off across the square.

Once she was at a safe distance, Olivia stopped and snapped a picture of the zombie.

"The *Boogle Bay Bugle* will buy this picture for sure!"

Otto followed Ducky Doodle to the shops along the docks.

"I hope he isn't going to march off a pier into the water," thought Otto.

Just then, Uncle Tooth came by. "Otto! You found Doodle!"

"I can't stop him," Otto said. "He's been zombified."

Suddenly, Doodle stopped by himself. He stood in front of Jack Whiskers' Nautical Supplies and Hardware Store.

"Must get treasure," he muttered, going inside. Otto and Tooth went in after him.

Doodle went straight to the shovels, grabbed one, and set it on his shoulder.

When he started to leave the shop, Jack Whiskers called, "Hey!"

Otto and Uncle Tooth grabbed Ducky Doodle. They pinned him to the ground. It was not easy. Doodle seemed to have developed double strength.

"The little thief!" Jack Whiskers said.

"It's not his fault. He's under a spell," said Uncle Tooth. "Still, I think it would be a good idea to place him in jail until we can figure out what's wrong with him."

They were leading Ducky Doodle along the street when Auntie Hick ran over. "Doodle! For mercy's sake! What's going on?"

"We caught him trying to steal a shovel

from the hardware store," said Uncle Tooth.

Auntie Hick gasped. "This is terrible! I'm sure someone put him up to it!"

"We agree," Otto told her. "Ducky Doodle isn't being punished. We're putting him in jail for his own good."

Auntie Hick came along to the jail. When they arrived, they found Olivia talking to Captain Poopdeck. "Guess what?" Olivia cried. "Madame Webster and a zombie named 'Clegg' tried to grab my camera!"

"Ha! Now do you believe me?" Otto said to Olivia.

"Yes. But I still don't want to be in your stupid club. So don't ask!"

Uncle Tooth raised his hand for silence. "First, let's get Ducky Doodle in a cell. Then I want to hear all about what's going on."

4
FULL MOON AND TEA LEAVES

Ducky Doodle was safely shut in a cell. Uncle Tooth lit his pipe and sat down to hear Otto's and Olivia's stories. Captain Poopdeck had a story of his own. At least four other people had been reported missing!

"I think it's time we *all* went over to Triangular Square," Uncle Tooth said.

Captain Poopdeck couldn't come. He had to go check out another missing person.

Auntie Hick insisted on keeping Ducky Doodle company. She couldn't bear to leave him alone in such a state, even if he didn't know her.

Otto, Uncle Tooth, and Olivia set forth. The sky had turned steely gray. Patches of black clouds rolled on a steady wind.

"Uncle Tooth, what exactly *is* a zombie?" Olivia said.

"Glad you asked," answered Uncle Tooth. "A zombie is a person who isn't a person anymore. Their spirit has been stolen. The person who holds the zombie's spirit can make the zombie do whatever they want. By the way, it was smart of you to take pictures. We need all the evidence we can get."

"What about *my* evidence?" cried Otto. "It was my idea to check out the shop to begin with. If I hadn't seen the zombie first, you'd never..."

Uncle Tooth broke in. "Otto, there will be

no more arguing. If we want to get to the bottom of this, we all have to work together. Your part is just as important as everybody else's. Now, can I count on you?"

"I guess so."

"Excuse me?"

"I mean...Yes! You can count on me."

"Excellent!" said Uncle Tooth.

They stopped in a doorway across the street from 1313 Triangular Square. "I know that place," whispered Uncle Tooth. "It used to be the old button shop."

Uncle Tooth was a man of action. He marched over and knocked on the door so hard that Otto jumped. Olivia aimed her camera. She was ready to snap a picture of whoever answered the door.

Uncle Tooth knocked again. He gave the door a kick and it swung open.

The shop was dark. It appeared to be empty.

The three entered slowly.

"Is anybody here?" called Uncle Tooth.

Silence.

Olivia checked the closets. Uncle Tooth looked behind the counter. Otto explored the back.

Suddenly, Olivia let out a piercing scream.

Sedley Mether was standing inside a closet with a blank look on his face.

Uncle Tooth rushed forward and waved his hand in front of Sedley's face.

"He's been zombified, all right."

"Come see what I found!" Otto called.

Olivia ran back and snapped a picture.

Otto blinked at the flash. "Will you knock it off?" he said. "It's just me.

"Look," said Otto. He pointed to a round table set between two chairs. "Someone has been drinking tea."

On the table were two cups and a teapot. One of the cups was clean. The other had tea leaves at the bottom.

"Fortune-tellers use tea leaves to read fortunes," Olivia told Otto. "I thought everyone knew that."

"No, Otto's on to something," said Uncle Tooth. He picked up the used cup and gave it a sniff. "Otto, you may have found just the thing we've been looking for."

"I don't see how," said Olivia.

"Unless I'm very much mistaken, these

leaves are the kind used to brew Zombie Tea. It turns people into zombies," Uncle Tooth explained. "The leaves only grow in one place I know of: Mookey Swamp, home of the Cobweb Queen!"

"The Cobweb Queen!" cried Otto. "Do you think she's involved in this?"

Uncle Tooth nodded. "I'm sure of it. In fact, I believe Madame Webster *is* the Cobweb Queen. I found these behind the counter."

He held up a pair of dark glasses and a frizzy wig.

Otto smiled. "I can see the headlines now: OTTO CRACKS ZOMBIE CASE."

"Get over it," replied Olivia.

Suddenly, they heard flute music somewhere in the distance.

"What eerie music," said Olivia. "It makes my flesh creep."

Otto was about to say something nasty when he realized that his flesh felt creepy, too. "Hey!" he cried. "There goes Sedley!"

Charmed by the music, Sedley Mether walked out the open door and down the street. Otto, Uncle Tooth, and Olivia went after him.

They saw Sedley joining a line of people, all following the creepy music.

"Zombies!" exclaimed Uncle Tooth.

At the jail, Auntie Hick tried talking to Ducky Doodle. But it was hopeless. He just stared straight ahead. Every so often, he would mutter, "Treasure...must find treasure."

It was all rather spooky.

When she glanced out the window, Auntie Hick saw a large full moon pop from behind some clouds. She heard flute music nearby. Such creepy music!

Doodle perked up. He began shaking the bars of his cell.

"This is too much!" Auntie Hick muttered.

There was a knock on the jail door. Thinking it was Captain Poopdeck, she ran and flung the door open. Auntie Hick found herself staring into the eyes of a large creature. Next to the creature stood the Cobweb Queen, with a flute in her hand.

"I've come for my zombie," she said.

Auntie Hick fainted.

Dozens of zombies were marching along the docks. They came from alleyways and houses. Some even came off ships. All were following the sound of the Cobweb Queen's flute.

Horrified, Otto, Uncle Tooth, and Olivia made their way past the zombies to the jail.

The bars on Doodle's cell had been bent back. Doodle and Auntie Hick were gone!

They ran outside. By now, the line of zombies had reached the edge of town. It was disappearing into Mookey Swamp. One especially large zombie was carrying Auntie Hick.

"Clegg!" cried Olivia.

"We've got to stop them!" screamed Otto.

Uncle Tooth sighed. "I'm afraid that's impossible. The spell has given the zombies superhuman strength."

"But we can't just let them take Ducky Doodle and Auntie Hick," said Olivia.

"Of course we can't," Uncle Tooth replied. "But it's too dark to head into the swamp now. Olivia, you come spend the night at our house. We'll get a fresh start in the morning."

"This is going to be a scary adventure, isn't it?" Otto asked.

Uncle Tooth nodded. "It already is."

That night, before crawling beneath the covers, Otto locked his bedroom window and put his Good-Luck Pebble under his pillow.

Somehow, saying "I told you so" to Olivia hadn't been nearly as much fun as Otto imagined it would be.

5
INTO THE SWAMP

The next morning, they formed a zombie posse.

Uncle Tooth brought a coil of rope, a flashlight, and his trusty wooden sword. Otto brought his slingshot and his Good-Luck Pebble. Olivia brought her camera.

"That should be real effective in fighting zombies," Otto said.

"Who said anything about *fighting* them?" answered Olivia. "I'm going to photograph them for the *Boogle Bay Bugle*."

Otto laughed. "I can't wait to see the one

of the zombie dragging you into the swamp. That should make the front page. Too bad you won't be around to see it."

"We'll see," said Olivia.

"Olivia's right," Uncle Tooth said. "It's pointless to try and fight the zombies. The Queen's magic has made them strong, and there are too many of them."

"So how do we stop them?" asked Otto.

"*That's* the mystery we have to solve," said Uncle Tooth.

Captain Poopdeck and Jack Whiskers were going to stay in Boogle Bay in case any zombies returned.

"We're counting on you," Captain Poopdeck told them. "Good luck."

Otto felt for the pebble in his pocket and gave it a squeeze. Olivia snapped a picture of everybody, and the zombie posse set forth.

They entered Mookey Swamp. Right away, the air became heavy and damp. The cries of unseen birds echoed through the gloom.

The swamp was a dangerous place, with or without zombies. There were holes to fall into, twisted roots to trip over, and vines to get caught in. It was home to the spinning Kootcha Bugs and the vicious Eenie Meanies. No one ever went on picnics in Mookey Swamp!

To keep their spirits up, Uncle Tooth

taught Otto and Olivia a zombie chant.

"This was given to me years ago by the sorceress Madame Ornithon," he said. "She was part buzzard, part loon, and all magic. But it was *good* magic.

> "We will face the fearful zombies.
> We will look them in the eye.
> We won't let the evil scare us.
> We are strong enough to try!"

They walked along singing until their throats got dry. Uncle Tooth had wisely brought a Thermos of lemonade. They took turns drinking from it.

Otto asked, "If we can't find out how to break the spell, will Ducky Doodle and Sedley Mether have to stay zombies forever?"

"Not as long as my name is Uncle Tooth!" said Uncle Tooth.

"I see one!" cried Olivia. Olivia flashed her camera.

It turned out to be only an old sign peeking through some bushes. It said: PIRATE'S GRAVEYARD.

"Geesh!" said Otto. "Do you have to be so loud? You scared the life out of me!"

"I wouldn't say that in a graveyard, if I were you," replied Olivia.

She walked into the thick grass and began to read the headstones.

Suddenly, a rock whizzed past her and bounced off a tree. "Otto, stop that!" she yelled.

Another rock flew past Otto's head. He ducked.

"We're being attacked!" he cried.

Uncle Tooth crouched down next to him.

A third rock fell to earth with a thud.

"Go away, you zombies!" called a voice.

"We're not zombies!" Uncle Tooth called back.

It did no good. The rocks kept flying.

"They're coming from that shack," Otto whispered. "I'll try to sneak up on whoever it is."

"Stay close to the ground," Uncle Tooth whispered back.

Otto nodded and crawled away.

"We don't mean you any harm," Uncle Tooth called.

"That's what they *all* say," came the voice. Another rock shot over.

"You'd better not hit my camera, or I'll come over there and kick your butt," said Olivia.

The thrower said, "Why would a *zombie* have a camera?"

By now, Otto had reached the shack.

On the porch, he saw an old sailor, surrounded by a pile of rocks, bottles, and bricks.

Otto fitted a stone into his slingshot, just
as the sailor prepared to toss a bottle.

BING!—he knocked the bottle from the sailor's hand.

"Now!" cried Otto.

Uncle Tooth rushed forward and pounced on the old fellow. There was a furious tussle, but the sailor was no match for Uncle Tooth. In no time, Uncle Tooth had him tied up.

"This is the last straw!" shouted the sailor. "If it ain't zombies, it's thieves!"

"We're not thieves," Olivia told him.

"But we won't untie you until you explain why you were throwing rocks at us," Uncle Tooth added.

The old sailor looked suspiciously from Otto to Tooth to Olivia.

Finally, he sighed and said, "Very well."

6
COPPER BILL'S TALE

"My name is Copper Bill. This place used to be a pirate hangout. There are caves to camp in and a lagoon for docking ships. But for as long as I can remember, it's been abandoned. For the last six years, I've lived here with my daughter, Little Effie. It's a lonely life, but we like it. At least we did until about a week ago.

"That was when this weird woman and her friend, a patch-eyed parrot, moved into the old mansion round back. People say it used to be the home of a zombie priestess.

"The strangers took a peculiar interest in

Little Effie. They said how small she was and how good she would be at getting in and out of tight places. They tried to get her to visit them in the mansion. But I wouldn't allow it. Still, you know how stubborn children are— no offense intended. One morning, Little Effie was gone!

"I looked everywhere for her. When I went toward the mansion, the trees were filled with snakes and bats and I couldn't get through. Sadly, I returned home.

"As I brewed a cup of coffee and pondered my next move, there was a creak on the porch. I opened the door and saw Little Effie standing there—or, what *used* to be Little Effie. They had turned her into a hideous zombie!

"I brought her in and set her before the fire. I tried talking to her, but it was as if her brains were stuffed with cornbread. She just

sat there, not speaking. Then I heard organ music coming from the old mansion. Creepy music. As soon as it started, Little Effie rose, walked out the door, and vanished into the swamp. I followed, but couldn't get past the snakes and bats.

"I was sick with grief. Last night, I saw the weird woman walking through the trees followed by a whole line of zombies! When I saw you, I thought you were zombies coming for *me* next."

7
LOST LUCK

Uncle Tooth untied Copper Bill.

"The zombies you saw last night are friends of ours," he said. "And that weird woman is the Cobweb Queen. If we're going to stop this zombie curse, we need you to show us where the mansion is."

"Gladly," said Copper Bill. "But you won't get past the snakes and bats."

Copper Bill led them through the Pirate's Graveyard, past the lagoon and pirate caves, to the darkest part of the swamp.

"Do you think the Cobweb Queen is searching for pirate treasure?" Olivia asked.

"She may be," said Copper Bill. "But if there was any treasure here, I bet it was dug up long ago. I think she's after something in the mansion. Something belonging to the zombie priestess."

"Like what?" asked Otto.

"Beats me," said Copper Bill.

He stopped and pointed to an opening. "Right in there. I hope you know what you're doing."

Uncle Tooth said, "We'll be all right. We have a zombie chant to help us."

"And my Good-Luck Pebble," said Otto. "Hey! Where is it?" He dug in the pocket of his sweater. "It's gone! Where..."

Suddenly, a chill ran through him.

"Oh, no! I used the pebble in my slingshot. How could I have been so stupid?"

"Just practice, I guess," said Olivia.

"The pebble was used for a good cause," said Uncle Tooth.

"But I need it for protection!" Otto cried. "You don't understand!"

"*I* understand you're acting like a baby," said Olivia.

"What do *you* know? You and that stupid camera! I wish you'd never come to Boogle Bay!"

"Otto! That's enough," Uncle Tooth said firmly. "There's no reason to attack Olivia. Now listen to me."

He knelt and placed a hand on Otto's shoulder. "A lucky object is easy to lose. But you have something that can never be lost unless you choose to lose it."

"What's that?" sniffed Otto.

"Your own courage. A pebble can't stand up to the Queen. You can. If you used the pebble in your slingshot, it's because you don't need it anymore."

Otto thought about this. "You think so?"

"I'm sure of it," said Uncle Tooth.

Copper Bill wiped a tear from his eye. "Dang! It's as if you were talking to me. I've let my fear of the snakes and bats hold me back from going after Little Effie. I have courage, too, and I want to use it."

"Excellent!" said Uncle Tooth.

He turned to Olivia. "And I'd like a little more sympathy from you, young lady. We all need to stick together at a time like this."

"Sorry," said Olivia. "It won't happen again."

8
SNAKES AND BATS

Halfway down the path, a band of bats came out of nowhere and flew at their faces. Our heroes swatted at them blindly.

Uncle Tooth aimed his flashlight at the bats. Presto!

They turned out to be nothing but dried leaves!

"Tricks! All tricks!" Uncle Tooth huffed.

"Watch out!" shouted Copper Bill.

A mean-looking snake was curling down a tree branch toward Olivia's neck.

Uncle Tooth sprang forward. He grabbed the snake in both hands and flung it to the ground. He hacked at it with his sword.

"Look. It isn't a snake at all!" cried Otto.

Uncle Tooth held up his sword.

Dangling from it was a long, limp vine.

"More tricks! This time, she even had *me* fooled," he said.

In the confusion, Uncle Tooth dropped his flashlight. The swamp ooze sucked it up. Otto felt helpless, until he remembered his courage. "If a Good-Luck Pebble can't stand up to the Cobweb Queen, I guess a flashlight can't either," he thought.

Just ahead, the mansion loomed eerily. Uncle Tooth snorted. "This looks like zombie territory, all right!"

A crew of zombies was digging up the grounds in spooky silence. Watching over them was One-Eyed Eddy, the Cobweb Queen's parrot.

"Dig faster, you zombies!" he ordered. "Or I may have to use my whip."

Olivia shuddered. "The swine!"

"Do you see Little Effie?" Otto asked Copper Bill.

"Nope. She must be inside. I hope they haven't forced her into some small space she can't get out of." Copper Bill removed his cap and scratched his head.

"I have an idea. Suppose I enter the yard walking like a zombie," Bill said. "The zombies won't notice. But that parrot probably will. While he's looking at me, you three try to get inside the mansion."

"Good plan," said Uncle Tooth.

It *was* a good plan. One-Eyed Eddy did notice Copper Bill. Bill sped up his zombie

walk and led the parrot on a merry chase.

Otto, Uncle Tooth, and Olivia snuck past the zombies to the side of the mansion. Uncle Tooth tried the front door. Otto and Olivia went to check for other ways in.

The back door had boards nailed across it. But they found an open basement window.

Otto paused to gather pebbles for his slingshot. Olivia started to crawl in through the window. Suddenly, she heard Otto scream. She spun around to see him in the clutches of the huge zombie, Clegg!

9
SPIDERS!

If only Olivia had brought a weapon...but maybe she had!

She ran forward and flashed her camera in the zombie's face.

He groaned, blinked his eyes, and tottered about. Otto slipped free!

"Thanks. I owe you one," Otto said.

They crawled through the basement window.

It was dark and smelly and cobwebby down there. There were some coffins, all empty, and in one corner, a bunch of cereal boxes.

Olivia set her camera on a shelf while she

bent down to examine a small rug. Suddenly, she screamed.

"GAA! Spiders! They're crawling all over me! Get off! Get off!"

Otto grabbed Olivia's camera, aimed at the rug, and flashed.

"They're gone," said Olivia.

"No," said Otto. "They're in the rug—see? Only they aren't real. They're just sewn in the design."

"Tricks again," said Olivia. She took her camera back. "I would have figured that out myself. You didn't have to go wasting film."

"I was just trying to help," said Otto. "Some thanks I get! From now on, you're on your own!" He stomped up some stairs.

Olivia stayed behind. She spied a door across the room that she wanted to check out.

Meanwhile, Uncle Tooth had got in easily through the mansion's front door. He stood in the main hall. There wasn't even a zombie on guard. "The Queen's got them all working," he thought.

He saw someone and jumped!

It was only his reflection in a large mirror.

In the mirror, he saw the front door opening. One-Eyed Eddy came in.

Uncle Tooth ducked behind a pipe organ.

One-Eyed Eddy looked around the room. Then he headed for a swinging door.

Uncle Tooth slipped from his hiding place

and followed. The door led to a long hallway lined with old oil paintings. Uncle Tooth saw Eddy slip behind a curtain.

The moment Uncle Tooth went through the swinging door, Otto came up from the basement.

He also jumped when he saw himself reflected in the large mirror. He jumped again when he saw Clegg peering at him through a window.

Backing up against the mirror, Otto tried to summon his courage. In an instant, the mirror swung around, like a door at the Fun House!

Otto found himself in another room. "Whew—that was close!" he thought.

In front of him, a staircase wound up into the darkness. Taking a breath, Otto mounted the stairs, slingshot at the ready.

10
THE QUEEN'S PLAN

Meanwhile, Olivia had opened the door in the basement and discovered Auntie Hick. She was bound to a chair and gagged. Olivia untied her.

"Olivia!" Auntie Hick said. "I knew you'd come. That evil witch tried to make me drink some of her wretched tea. I refused...and you know what a tea lover I am!"

Auntie Hick was trembling.

"Get a grip on yourself, Auntie Hick. Do you know where Ducky Doodle is?"

"No," said Auntie Hick, getting slowly to her feet. "But we'll find him."

Uncle Tooth was hiding behind a curtain, listening to Eddy and the Cobweb Queen.

The Queen lay on a sofa. Sedley Mether stood a few feet away, painting her picture.

"Eddy, tell me. Does it look like me?"

Eddy leaned over to peer at the picture. Sedley Mether hadn't painted the Queen. He had painted a large sunflower instead.

"It's you, all right," said Eddy. "Listen, about the zombies..."

"They haven't stopped working, have they?"

"No, it's just that one of 'em was moving so fast I couldn't catch him."

"You're not supposed to catch them," answered the Queen. "You're supposed to make them work. Have you been telling them to work faster?"

"Well, yes...but..."

"That's the beauty of zombies. They always do exactly what you tell them. Paint faster!" she commanded Sedley.

The Queen rose and began pacing. "At this rate, they'll uncover the Silver Skull in no time. Then all the Zombie Priestess's power will be mine! With that skull and an army of zombies, I'll be unstoppable!"

Uncle Tooth burst through the curtain, waving his wooden sword.

"So that's your game plan!" he shouted.

"Tooth!" shrieked the Queen. "Typical of you to drop by without an invitation. Can I offer you some tea?"

"I don't want your tea! I want my friends returned to normal!"

"Can't do that," said the Queen. "I need them to help me rule the world. Cheap labor is so hard to come by these days."

Eddy laughed. "I've got a whip here," he told Uncle Tooth, "so lower your sword."

"Wait a minute!" cried the Queen. "Tooth, surely you didn't come here alone. Where's that pesky nephew of yours?"

"They could have a whole army, for all we know," added Eddy.

"No matter," the Queen laughed. "*We* have an army. An army of zombies!"

11
A LITTLE ORGAN MUSIC

Otto reached the top of the winding staircase. He found himself in a laboratory. A big pot of Zombie Tea was bubbling. On one shelf were bottles of dried leaves in all colors and sizes. On another shelf were some jars with stoppers.

Each jar had a label with the name of a person written on it. What could *that* mean? The first one Otto picked up said LITTLE EFFIE.

Otto heard a noise behind him. He spun around.

There stood a freaky-looking girl with dark eyes and blue skin. A zombie!

Otto dropped the jar. It smashed on the tile floor. From the broken bits arose a green mist. It drifted into the zombie's eyes.

The next instant, the zombie was gone!

Standing in its place was a little girl with a confused expression. "What happened?" she asked. "Who are you?"

"I-I'm Otto. Who are you?"

"My name is Little Effie," the girl said. "The last thing I remember is some old woman

forcing me to drink some yucky-tasting tea."

"*You're* Little Effie?" cried Otto. "This is wonderful! Do you know what this means? When I dropped that jar with your name on it, the zombie spell was broken."

He led her to the shelf and showed her the other jars. "These jars must contain all the zombies' spirits. Little Effie, peek out that door and see where it leads." Otto pointed to a door opposite the stairs.

"It leads to a hallway with a balcony at the end," Little Effie said.

"Perfect," said Otto. "If you want to get out of this spooky place, I need your help."

Olivia and Auntie Hick came up from the basement just in time to see the Cobweb Queen and One-Eyed Eddy leading Uncle Tooth into the main hall.

"Aha!" cried the Queen. "Thought you could escape, huh? I'm way ahead of you."

"What have you done with Ducky Doodle?" demanded Auntie Hick.

Copper Bill appeared through another door. "What have you done with Little Effie?"

"See for yourselves," the Queen answered.

With a swish of her cape, she seated herself at the organ and began to play an eerie tune. "Ah, who can resist my zombie music? I found this sheet music in the basement. It's quite charming, really."

Auntie Hick rushed forward, snatched the sheet music, and tore it to shreds.

"Now you've really irritated me!" hissed the Queen. "But it doesn't matter...see?"

From all around, doors were opening and zombies were entering the room.

12
TOO MANY ZOMBIES

Among the zombies was Ducky Doodle.

"My poor Doodle! This is hideous!" cried Auntie Hick.

"I'm afraid he can't hear you," said the Queen. "*I* should be so lucky."

The zombies moved closer and closer.

Soon, they had Uncle Tooth, Copper Bill, Olivia, and Auntie Hick surrounded. Auntie Hick started trembling again.

Uncle Tooth stepped forward and led them in the zombie chant:

"We will face the fearful zombies.
We will look them in the eye.
We won't let the evil scare us.
We are strong enough to try!"

SNAP! SNAP! SNAP! Olivia spun about
and flashed the zombies with her camera.

The zombies blinked their eyes. They
began to totter about.

"Hey! No funny stuff!" cried One-Eyed Eddy. "I've got a whip here!"

Uncle Tooth snatched the whip from Eddy. "No, you don't," he said.

Otto and Little Effie began tossing the jars over the balcony. The jars smashed on the carpet. For every one that broke, a zombie snapped out of his or her spell.

The former zombies stood about shaking their heads.

"Your little game is over," Uncle Tooth told the Queen. "You are the worst kind of thief. Most thieves steal only money or jewels. But you stole these people's spirits. Well, we don't believe in your power anymore."

The Cobweb Queen backed toward the organ. She pulled Eddy along with her.

"If there's one thing I hate worse than paying for labor, it's losing to cheaters!" she hissed. "*This* game may be over, but you'll find I have more up my sleeve than just my arm!"

She pressed a key on the organ. There was a puff of blue smoke. When it cleared, Eddy and the Cobweb Queen were gone!

"They've escaped through a trapdoor," said Uncle Tooth, bending down.

Suddenly, they heard the Queen's voice

echoing through the walls: "I'll get you when you're not looking, Tooth!"

"Not if I see you first," Uncle Tooth shot back.

Little Effie ran into Copper Bill's arms.

Auntie Hick grabbed Ducky Doodle and gave him a good squeeze.

Even Otto and Olivia hugged each other.

Sedley Mether walked into the room. He was holding up his sunflower painting.

"I must say, I think it's one of my better efforts. Only, I can't remember painting it. Say...how did we all get *here?*"

Uncle Tooth laughed. "We'll explain on the way back," he said.

13
HEROES

A few days later, Ducky Doodle, Olivia, and Auntie Hick were over at Otto and Uncle Tooth's house.

Uncle Tooth roasted some corn on the cob. Otto mixed up a big batch of lemonade, and Auntie Hick brought her famous rhubarb pie.

They sat outside and listened to the June bugs in the reeds. Boogle Bay was peaceful once again.

"I wonder where that Silver Skull the Cobweb Queen wanted is hidden," said Otto.

"I wonder if there even *is* such a thing,"

said Uncle Tooth. "Copper Bill promised to let me know if the Queen and Eddy come snooping around again. But if I know her, she's lost interest in the skull and is busy with some new scheme."

"I can't believe how brave you all were to come into the swamp," said Ducky Doodle.

"When you love someone, it's easy to be brave," Auntie Hick said.

"I was surprised I could still be brave, even without my Good-Luck Pebble," said Otto.

"I loved the part when you threw all the jars off the balcony," Olivia told him.

"Thanks," said Otto. "Your camera sure came in handy! That was fancy shooting!"

"You discovered how to stop the zombie curse," said Olivia. "I wanted to do that."

"I'm proud of *all* of you," Uncle Tooth said. "Things turn out better when everyone works together, don't you agree?"

"Yes...except *one* thing didn't turn out right," said Olivia. "My photos."

"Why not?" the others asked.

Olivia spread the photos. "See?" she said. "The bats look like leaves, the snakes look like vines, and the zombies look like people."

Uncle Tooth leaned back in his rocker, lit his pipe, and laughed. "Well, of course! In the light, the Cobweb Queen's magic just looks like stupid tricks!"

DON'T MISS THE NEXT GEOFFREY HAYES BOOK!

So everyone worked together to stop the zombies.

I tell you, it's enough to make me sick!

Fortunately, Otto and Olivia are fighting again. I like that in children.

They get lost in the deserted Fun House and discover that it's the home of ghosts. And not just any ghosts. These ghosts were once a band of cutthroats and thieves!

Now the ghosts are chasing our heroes past mazes, mirrors, and moving floors.

Will Otto and Olivia discover the secret of the Fun House in time?

Or will the horrible ghosts keep them trapped inside forever?

I'm not telling.

Read my next Creeper Mystery and find out for yourselves!

ABOUT THE AUTHOR

Geoffrey Hayes grew up in San Francisco, where he still lives. When he was a boy, Geoffrey and his brother Rory made up stories about their collection of stuffed animals.

When Geoffrey got older, he put some of these stories into books, like the one you've just read.

So far, he has written over thirty books for young readers.

When he isn't writing, Geoffrey likes to dance, go to movies, and play games on his computer.